My Weird School #3

Mrs. Roopy Is Loopy!

Dan Gutman

Pictures by
Jim Paillot

🅷 HarperTrophy®
An Imprint of HarperCollinsPublishers

Mrs. Roopy Is Loopy!
Text copyright © 2004 by Dan Gutman
Illustrations copyright © 2004 by Jim Paillot

Library of Congress Cataloging-in-Publication Data

Gutman, Dan.
  Mrs. Roopy is loopy! / Dan Gutman ; pictures by Jim Paillot –1st ed.
     p.   cm. – (My weird school ; #3)
  Summary: A.J. and his classmates are convinced that new school librarian, Mrs. Roopy,
has multiple personality disorder because she keeps pretending to be famous people.
  ISBN-0-06-050704-7 (pbk.)—ISBN-0-06-050705-5 (lib. bdg.)
  [1. Schools—Fiction. 2. Librarians—Fiction. 3. Learning—Fiction. 4. Humorous stories.]
I. Paillot, Jim, ill. II. Title. III. Series.
PZ7.G9846Mt 2004   2003024072
[Fic]—dc22

Typography by Nicole de las Heras
❖
Revised Harper Trophy edition, 2004
Visit us on the World Wide Web!
www.harperchildrens.com

09 10 11 12 13 LP/CW 20 19 18 17

To Emma

Contents

1	That Army Guy	1
2	The Librarian	7
3	George Washington's Teeth	14
4	Dumbheads	19
5	Mrs. Roopy's Hero	24
6	Johnny Applesauce	38
7	One Small Step for Man	43
8	Nursery Rhyme Week	50
9	Mrs. Roopy's Problem	59
10	The Evidence	63
11	Just Admit It!	71
12	The Proof	79

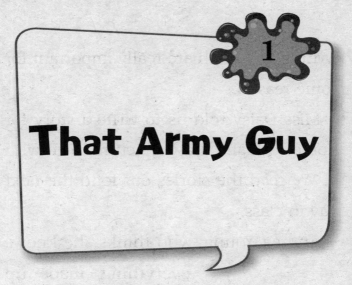

That Army Guy

My name is A.J. and I hate school.

If you ask me, they shouldn't teach kids how to read and write in school. They shouldn't teach math. They should teach kids how to do tricks on their bikes. That's what I want to learn! But my teacher, Miss Daisy, thinks reading and writing and math are really important for some reason.

Miss Daisy told us to write a story for homework and draw a picture to go with it. We read the stories out loud the next day in class.

Andrea Young, who thinks she knows everything, made up a story about a family of flowers who were sad because it was cloudy out-side. Then the sun came out and the flowers got happy again.

It was a really dumb story, if you ask me. Flowers aren't happy or sad. They just sit there and do nothing. They don't even have families! But Miss Daisy kept telling Andrea how great the story was.

My story was about these giant man-eating monsters fighting on trick bikes in

outer space until they were all dead. I drew cool pictures to go with it. Emily, this girl with red hair, said my story was scary. But Emily thinks everything is scary.

Miss Daisy said I had a good imagination, but she asked me if next time I could try to write a story that didn't have so much violence in it.

"What's violent about giant man-eating monsters fighting on trick bikes in outer space?" I asked. Everybody laughed even though I didn't say anything funny.

Andrea said maybe I could have the man-eating monsters make up at the end of the story and tell each other they were sorry.

"Monsters don't apologize!" I said.

Everybody knows that. Andrea doesn't know anything about monsters.

We were arguing about it when all of a sudden some funny-looking guy marched into our classroom. He was all dressed up

in a fancy army uniform. He had a white wig on his head and a sword in his hand.

"To be prepared for war is the best way to keep the peace!" the army guy said. Then he marched out of the classroom.

"Who was that?" asked my friend Michael, who never ties his shoes no matter how many times he trips over the laces.

"Beats me," I said.

"Was that Principal Klutz?" asked my other friend Ryan, who sits next to me in the third row.

"I don't know who it was," Miss Daisy said, "but he is heading for the library. We'd better go check it out! Okay, second graders. Single file!"

The Librarian

Michael was the line leader. Andrea was the door holder. We went to the library, which is brand-new and didn't even exist last year when we were in first grade. They built it over the summer to replace the junky old library we used to have.

A library is the part in the school where they have hundreds of books that you can bring home with you. You don't even have to pay for them. And it's not even illegal! The only problem is you have to bring the books back after you're done reading them.

My friend Billy around the corner, who was in second grade last year, told me that if you don't bring back your library books on time, the librarian locks you in a dungeon under the school. I'm not sure I believe him.

"Our new librarian is Mrs. Roopy," Miss Daisy told us as we lined up in the hall-way outside the library. "Everybody be on your best behavior so you'll make a good impression on her."

"I'm always on my best behavior," said

Andrea Young. She made a big dopey smile at Miss Daisy. Andrea is so annoying. If somebody told her to be on her worst behavior, she wouldn't know what to do.

When we went into the new library, we were shocked. Right in the middle of the room was a giant tree! It had a big tree house at the top near the ceiling and a ladder going up to it.

"What's with the tree?" I asked.

"Beats me," said Ryan. "How do you think they got it into the library?"

"Maybe it just grew in here over the summer," guessed Michael.

"Trees don't grow in libraries," said Andrea, as if she knows anything about trees.

"They must have built
it," said Emily.

"You don't build trees,
dumbhead," I told Emily,

and she looked all
hurt like she was
going to cry.

The tree was

really cool. Some of us started to climb it, but Miss Daisy said we had to get off because it was time for library period to start.

"Where's the new librarian?" Ryan

asked. We were all looking around, but we didn't see Mrs. Roopy anywhere.

Then, suddenly, that army guy with the wig poked his head out of the tree house. He came down the ladder. I think it was a he, anyway. He looked a little like a lady dressed like an army guy.

When he got to the bottom, the army guy with the wig stood all straight and proud at attention. He gave us a salute.

"Are you Mrs. Roopy?" I asked.

"Certainly not," the army guy said. "My name is George Washington. I am the first president of the United States and father of our country."

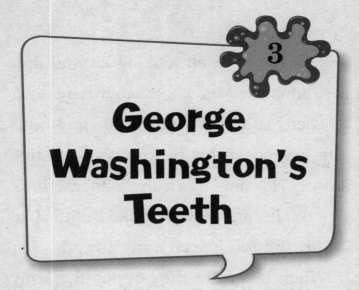

George Washington's Teeth

I'm no dumbhead. My mom told me that George Washington had wooden teeth. So this army guy with the wig couldn't be George Washington unless he had wooden teeth.

"If you're really George Washington, let's see your teeth," I said. The army guy with the wig reached into his pocket and pulled out a set of teeth. Then he wound a little thing on it and the teeth started chattering up and down in his hand.

Emily took one look at the teeth and ran out of the room crying. That girl cries at anything.

"Wow!" I said. "Maybe he is George Washington. Those teeth are cool! I wish I had wooden teeth."

"You can't fool me," Andrea Young said. "You're not George Washington. You're Mrs. Roopy, the new librarian, dressed up to look like George Washington. You're supposed to read stories to us and help us use the computers."

"Computers?" George Washington said, his forehead all wrinkly. "I don't know what you're talking about, young lady. This is the year 1790. Computers haven't been invented yet."

No matter what we said, the army guy with the wig insisted that he was really George Washington. He read us a story about when he was a boy and he chopped down a cherry tree. Then he showed us a bunch of books about the United States. All through library period, the army guy with the wig said that he was George Washington.

After a while, we started calling him George Washington.

"General Washington," I asked, "may I go to the bathroom?" Everybody laughed even though I didn't say anything funny. Kids think anything to do with bathrooms is funny. If you want to make your friends laugh, all you have to do is stick your face in their face and say either "bathroom" or "underwear." It works every time.

"I'm sorry," George Washington said. "This is the year 1790. Bathrooms have not been invented yet."

It wasn't an emergency or anything, so I waited. We were allowed to check out any book we wanted from the library. I took out a book about jet fighter planes because it had cool pictures in it.

For a president, this George Washington guy seemed to know a lot about finding books in the library and checking them out.

It was time to go to lunch. We all had to salute George Washington as we left the library.

"Hey, how come you chopped down that cherry tree, anyhow?" I asked him as we left the library.

"I cannot tell a lie," he said. "I needed some wood for my wooden teeth." Then he showed us his chattering teeth again. I'm still not sure if that army guy with the wig was George Washington or not. But he was weird.

Dumbheads

I took a seat in the lunchroom next to Ryan and Michael. Ryan stuck two of my carrot sticks in his nose, and I told him I'd give him a nickel if he ate them. He did, too. Me, I won't even eat carrot sticks *before* you stick them in your nose.

"Do you think that guy was really George Washington?" Ryan asked.

"I don't know," Michael said. "What do you think, A.J.?"

That's when Andrea Young leaned over from the next table and opened her big mouth.

"That wasn't George Washington, you dumbheads!" she said. "That was Mrs. Roopy wearing a powdered wig and an army uniform."

She may have been right, but I didn't want to admit it, because I hate her. Ryan took out a dollar bill from his backpack and looked at the picture of George Washington.

"He sure looked like George Washington," Ryan said.

"George Washington has been dead for like a hundred years!" Andrea said.

"Even if George Washington was still alive," Emily said, "I'm sure he would have more important things to do than come to our school and read us stories."

That's when it hit me. If that army guy was really Mrs. Roopy dressed up as George Washington, maybe Mrs. Roopy isn't a librarian at all!

"Maybe she's just pretending to be a librarian," I said, "just like she was pretending to be George Washington."

"Yeah!" Michael said. "Maybe she's a kidnapper and she's got our real librarian locked up in an empty warehouse at the edge of town. I saw that in a movie once."

"We've got to save her!" Emily said with

tears dribbling down her cheeks. Then she went running out of the room.

There was only one way to solve the problem. We cleaned off our trays and went back to our classroom to ask Miss Daisy if George Washington was really Mrs. Roopy in disguise.

"Don't be silly," Miss Daisy said. "As it turns out, Mrs. Roopy is absent today. She's home sick in bed. It must have been the real George Washington."

But what does Miss Daisy know? Everybody knows Miss Daisy is crazy.

Mrs. Roopy's Hero

Everybody in our class was excited before the next library period. We all wanted to see if George Washington would be there again.

When we got to the library, there was just this lady who looked a little bit like George Washington except she didn't have on an army uniform or a wig. She looked like a normal lady.

"Good morning, second graders," she said. "My name is Mrs. Roopy. I'm sorry I couldn't be here the other day for your library period."

"But you were here!" Ryan shouted.

"You must be

mistaken," Mrs. Roopy said. "I was home sick in bed."

"Can we see your wooden teeth again?" Michael asked.

"Yeah, can we?"

"Wooden teeth? Did you know that George Washington didn't have wooden teeth at all? His mouth was filled with cow's teeth."

"Ewww!" we all shouted.

I asked Mrs. Roopy, "Did the cow have George Washington's teeth in *her* mouth?"

"But that was you, wasn't it, acting like George Washington?" said Michael.

Mrs. Roopy's forehead got all wrinkly just like George Washington's did when we told him about computers. "I don't know what you're talking about."

We all looked at one another. I wasn't sure if she was telling the truth or not.

"If I were George Washington, would I have this?" Mrs. Roopy asked. Then she picked up her shirt and showed us her belly. She had a little tattoo of a heart right over her belly button. It was cool.

I had to admit that George Washington would never have a heart-shaped tattoo over his belly button. So maybe that army guy with the wig wasn't Mrs. Roopy after all.

"Let me show you around the library," Mrs. Roopy said. "Did you know that books can take you to places you have never been before? They help us explore our world. We have books here on just about every subject you can think of. This is the fiction section. Does anyone know the difference between fiction and nonfiction books?"

"Nonfiction books are books that are not fiction," Ryan said. "Because 'non' means *not*, like nonfat milk has no fat in it."

"And nonsense has no sense in it," Michael added.

"That's true," Mrs. Roopy said, "but there's a little more to it."

"Fiction is what you get when you rub two things together," I said.

Everybody laughed even though I didn't say anything funny.

"That's friction, A.J.," Andrea Young said. "Fiction is a made-up story, and non-fiction is based on facts."

"That's correct," said Mrs. Roopy, and she smiled at Andrea. I wished Andrea would shut up.

"Oh, who cares what the difference between fiction and nonfiction is?" I said. "All books are boring."

Everybody went "Oooooooh!" like I had said something really terrible.

"But everybody needs to know how to read, A.J.," Mrs. Roopy said.

"Not me," I said. "When I grow up, I'm going to be a trick bike rider because you don't have to know how to read to do tricks on a bike."

"Yeah, me too," said Michael and Ryan. We told Mrs. Roopy that, every day after school, me and Michael and Ryan ride our bikes together. I learned how to ride a two-wheeler in kindergarten. Now I can do a bunny hop off a bump, and I know the names of all the famous trick bike riders. I have posters of them all over the walls of my room.

"Gee, I don't know much about bicycle tricks, A.J.," Mrs. Roopy said. "But I've got posters of my hero on my walls at home too."

"Who is your hero, Mrs. Roopy?" Andrea asked.

"Melvil Dewey."

"Melvil Whoey?" I asked.

"Melvil Dewey was a very famous librarian," Mrs. Roopy said, and her eyes got all bright and sparkly and excited.

"Librarians aren't famous," I said.

"Melvil Dewey was," said Mrs. Roopy. "He invented the number system we use to find books in the library. If it weren't for Melvil Dewey, we would never be able to find anything."

"Wow!" Andrea Young said, as if she was really interested in that boring stuff.

"So if you want to find books about insects, you'd go to number 595," Mrs. Roopy said. "And if you want to find books about dinosaurs, you'd go to number 567. Libraries all over the world use the system that Melvil Dewey invented. Today we call it the Dewey decimal system."

"Did all the kids at his school make fun of him because his name was Melvil?" I asked. I know that if there was a kid named Melvil in our school, we would make fun of him constantly.

"I don't know," Mrs. Roopy said. "But would you like to hear a song I made up about Melvil Dewey?"

"Yeah!" we all shouted. Listening to songs had to be better than reading books.

Mrs. Roopy went into her office and came back with a guitar and one of those harmonica thingys you wear around your neck. She strummed a few chords to warm up.

"You may have heard a folktale about John Henry, the steel-drivin' man," Mrs. Roopy said. "Well, this is the story of Melvil Dewey, the book-sortin' man."

And then she started to sing. . . .

When Melvil Dewey was a little bitty
*   baby,*
The first words he said himself
Were "I've got to get these books off the
*   floor*
And put them on the shelf. . . ."

Mrs. Roopy sang the whole song and played her guitar and harmonica, too. It was a pretty cool song. This Melvil Dewey guy had a race with a computer to see who could sort books the fastest. Melvil won the race, but right after he sorted the last book, he dropped dead right on the floor of the library. It was cool.

At the end of the song, Andrea Young got up and gave Mrs. Roopy a standing ovation, so we all had to get up too.

"That's the saddest story I ever heard in my life," Emily said, wiping tears from her eyes.

At the end of the period, Mrs. Roopy asked us if we had any questions about how to use the library.

"Is it true that if we don't return our library books on time you lock us in a dungeon under the school?" I asked. Everybody laughed even though I didn't say anything funny.

"Don't be silly," Mrs. Roopy said. "The dungeon is on the third floor." I think she was telling a joke, but I'm not sure.

Johnny Applesauce

When we came into the library the next time, a guy with a long beard came down the ladder from the tree house, wearing blue-jean overalls. He was carrying a shovel and a big sack. He had no shoes on his feet, but he was wearing a pot on his head. He looked funny, and he looked a lot like Mrs. Roopy to me.

"Mrs. Roopy, why are you wearing a pot on your head?" I asked.

"Roopy?" the guy said in a funny voice. "You young 'uns must be confusin' me with some other feller. My name is Johnny Appleseed. It's the year 1800. I travel from

town to town plantin' apple trees most everywhere I wander."

"You are not Johnny Appleseed!" Andrea called out. "You're Mrs. Roopy!"

"Ain't never heard of no Roopy," the guy said, making his forehead all wrinkly. "Appleseed's the name. Plantin' apple trees is my game. This here's a darn big country, and I reckon folks are gonna need a heap of apples."

No matter what we said, we couldn't convince the bearded guy with the pot on his head that he wasn't Johnny Appleseed. He read us a story about Johnny Appleseed and told us lots of stuff about apples.

"Did you know that folks have been eatin' apples for thousands of years?" Johnny Appleseed told us.

"They should chew faster," I said, and everybody laughed.

Then Johnny Appleseed took us outside and helped us plant a real apple tree near the playground. Before we went back into school, we had apples for snack.

I can understand why he planted all those apple trees. I can understand why he was dressed funny. But what I don't understand is why he wore a pot on his head. That Johnny Applesauce guy was weird.

When we got back to class, I told Miss

Daisy all about what happened during library period.

"Do you still think books are boring, A.J.?" she asked me.

"Yes," I said.

One Small Step for Man

By this time, we weren't sure if Johnny Appleseed and George Washington had been to our school, or if it was just Mrs. Roopy dressed up in funny costumes. But we were sure of one thing.

Mrs. Roopy is loopy!

"We have to have proof," Michael said.

"My father is a policeman, and he said that if you want to be sure of something, you have to have proof. He always says the proof is in the pudding."

"What does pudding have to do with it?" I asked.

"Beats me," said Michael.

"Your dad is weird," I said.

"How are we going to prove that Mrs. Roopy is dressing up in funny costumes?" Ryan asked.

"We'll get her fingerprints!" Michael said, all excited. "That's what my dad does. Everybody in the whole world has different fingerprints. If we get Johnny Appleseed's fingerprints and then we get

Mrs. Roopy's fingerprints, I can have my dad test them. If they are the same fingerprints, then that will be proof that Mrs. Roopy was just pretending to be Johnny Appleseed!"

Me and Ryan agreed that Michael was a genius. The next time we had library, we brought a juice box with us, so we could get Mrs. Roopy's fingerprints.

But when we came into the library, all the lights were out and the shades were down. It was really dark. At first we thought the library was closed. Then we heard a noise. It came from the top of the tree house. We all looked up.

Somebody was coming down the

ladder. Whoever it was had on a spacesuit and was moving in slow motion. Some music began playing over the loudspeaker. "The *Eagle* . . . has landed," the astronaut said. Finally the astronaut reached the bottom rung of the ladder. It was hard to see a face through the space helmet.

"It's got to be Mrs. Roopy!" Andrea said.

"I'm not Mrs. Roopy," the astronaut said. "My name is Neil Armstrong. It is 1969. I am about to

become the first human being to set foot on the moon."

Slowly Neil Armstrong put one foot on the floor of the library.

"That's one small step for man, one giant leap for mankind," he said.

We tried to convince Neil Armstrong that he was really Mrs. Roopy dressed in a spacesuit, but he kept saying he had never heard of anyone named Roopy. Neil Armstrong spent the rest of the period showing us books about the moon and the sun and the stars and outer space. It was almost not boring, but not quite.

"Would you like some juice, Mr. Armstrong?" Michael asked, holding out the juice box.

"No thank you," Neil Armstrong said. "I've got to be getting back to Earth now. And I believe you have to go back to Miss Daisy's class."

Then he climbed up the ladder and into the tree house. Michael was disappointed that he didn't get Neil Armstrong's fingerprints.

When we got back to class, I told Miss Daisy all about Neil Armstrong stepping on the surface of the moon for the first time.

"Wow, that sounds exciting!" Miss Daisy said. "Do you still think books are boring, A.J.?"

"Yes," I said.

Nursery Rhyme Week

The only way to prove that Mrs. Roopy was dressing up in silly costumes and pretending to be other people would be to get her fingerprints. Me and Ryan and Michael were determined to get them the next time we had library.

"When do we have library this week?" we asked Miss Daisy.

"Oh, there is no library this week," she said. "The whole school is celebrating Nursery Rhyme Week in our classrooms."

"Oh man!" I said. "We wanted to go to the library."

"Yeah," agreed Michael and Ryan.

Miss Daisy looked all surprised. She put her hand on my forehead the way my mom does when she thinks I have a fever.

"Are you sick, A.J.?" Miss Daisy said. "There must be something wrong with you if you want to go to the library. Didn't you say all books are boring?"

"They are," I said. "I just want proof that Mrs. Roopy was pretending to be George Washington, Johnny Apple-seed, and Neil Armstrong. We have to get her fingerprints."

"Oh, don't be silly," Miss Daisy said. "Mrs. Roopy is a perfectly normal lady."

Miss Daisy took out a big fat Mother Goose book. She opened it and was about to start reading when this weird-looking girl skipped into the classroom. She was all dressed up in a puffy dress and she was holding a big cane.

"It's Mrs. Roopy!" we all shouted.

"I'm not Mrs. Roopy," the girl said. "My name is Little Bo Peep. I seem to have lost my sheep. Do you know where I can find them?"

"Nope," everybody said.

"Maybe they're in the dungeon on the

third floor," I said.

Michael tried to get her fingerprints, but Little Bo Peep went skipping out of the classroom before he could get a juice box.

"That was weird," Emily said.

"What kind of a name is Peep, anyway?" I asked.

Miss Daisy read us some nursery rhymes from the Mother Goose book. What kind of a name is Goose, anyway?

After a while, this other girl came running into our classroom. She was holding a bucket in her hand.

"It's Mrs. Roopy again!" we all shouted.

"Who are you now, Mrs. Roopy?" Emily asked.

"I'm not Mrs. Roopy," the girl said. "My name is Jill. I ran up a hill with my friend Jack to fetch a pail of water. But Jack fell down and broke his crown. I went running after him, but now I have no idea where he is. Have you seen him?"

"Nope," everybody said.

"Try the dungeon on the third floor," I said.

"You must be thirsty from all that running," Michael said. "Have some juice."

"No time for that," Jill said. "I've got to find Jack." And then she ran out of the classroom.

After lunch we were at recess out in the playground when we noticed somebody sitting at the edge of the grass under a tree. We all ran over to investigate. It was Mrs. Roopy, of course, dressed up in another silly costume.

"Are you Little Bo Peep again?" Emily asked.

"Heavens, no!" said Mrs. Roopy. "My

name is Little Miss Muffet. It's a lovely day, so I thought I'd just sit on this tuffet and eat some curds and whey."

"What's a tuffet?" I asked, trying to peek under Miss Muffet.

"What's a curd?" asked Ryan.

"Yuck," Michael said. "Curds sound disgusting!"

"I'm going to throw up," Ryan said. "That's even worse than what they serve in the cafeteria!"

"Wouldn't you rather have a peanut butter and jelly sandwich?" I asked.

Andrea and Emily came over while we were talking with Little Miss Muffet. Andrea started to tell us what curds and whey and tuffets were, but she never got to finish. This obviously fake spider came down from the tree over Miss Muffet's head. She took one look at it and ran back to school. Michael didn't even have the chance to get her fingerprints.

That lady is weird.

It went on like that for the rest of the week. All these nursery rhyme characters kept popping up with no warning

all over the school.

"Who are you now?" we would ask.

"I'm an old woman in a shoe. I have so many children I don't know what to do."

"Maybe you should put some of them in the dungeon on the third floor," I said.

In the next few days we were visited by Wee Willie Winkie, Georgie Porgie, Tommy Tucker, Simple Simon, Peter Peter Pumpkin Eater, and some guy named Jack who kept jumping over a candlestick for no reason at all. I guess it was the same Jack that girl Jill was looking for.

It was nonstop all week! I can't say for sure, but I'm pretty sure at least some of those nursery-rhyme characters were actually Mrs. Roopy.

Mrs. Roopy's Problem

Something was wrong with Andrea. She wasn't raising her hand in class every second. She wasn't bragging to everybody how much she knew about everything. She wasn't pestering me like she usually did. It was like she was sick or something.

"What's the matter, Andrea?" Emily asked her during recess.

"I'm worried about Mrs. Roopy," Andrea said. "I'm afraid she might have a serious personal problem."

"You're the one with the serious personal problem," I said. "Mrs. Roopy is like the coolest lady in the history of the world. Would you rather have some boring librarian who didn't dress up in

costumes or anything and all she did was read boring books to us?"

"No, but my mother is a psychologist," Andrea said. "She told me that some sick people have more than one personality. Like one minute they think they are one person, and a minute later they actually think they are somebody completely different. The whole time they actually think they are all these people. I'm afraid that Mrs. Roopy might have this problem. She can't tell the difference between the real world and fantasy."

"Wow," Michael said. "That sounds pretty serious."

"We've got to help her!" Emily said.

"Yeah," I said. "A librarian who doesn't know the difference between fiction and nonfiction is in big trouble."

"But what can we do?" Ryan asked.

We all put on our thinking caps. Well, not really. There's no such thing as a thinking cap. But you know what I mean.

After a good long think, I came up with a great plan.

The Evidence

There were five minutes left in recess. Ryan, Michael, Andrea, Emily, and I sneaked in from the playground through the door to the library.

"Shhhhh!" I said as we tiptoed into the library. "Follow me."

Lucky for us, the library was empty. Mrs. Roopy was probably eating lunch in the teachers' room.

On our hands and knees, we made our way past the nonfiction books to Mrs. Roopy's office. The door was unlocked. I opened it.

"We're going to get caught," Emily said.

"We're going to be kicked out of school and thrown in jail for the rest of our lives."

"In here," I said, ignoring Emily. "This is where we'll find the evidence."

We were inside Mrs. Roopy's office. I wanted to turn the light on, but Michael told me that when his father is doing a secret investigation, he never turns the lights on. We tried to see the best we could with the light that came in through the window.

"Do you see any evidence?" Michael said.

"Not yet."

It was just a bunch of boring stuff.

Pictures of Mrs. Roopy's daughter. Papers. Videos. Junk. No evidence at all.

"Let's get out of here," Emily said. "I'm scared."

"Not yet," I said.

There was a closet by the corner. I pulled the handle. It wasn't locked.

And there, inside the closet, was all the evidence we would ever need. George Washington's uniform. Little Bo Peep's dress. Johnny Appleseed's overalls. Neil Armstrong's spacesuit. Every single costume Mrs. Roopy had been wearing was hanging right there in the closet.

"This is the proof!" Michael said. "All those people were just Mrs. Roopy dressed up in costumes."

"I told you so," said Andrea.

"You did not!" I said.

"Did too!" she said.

"Oh, you think you know everything!" I said. "Well, you're not so smart!"

That's when the light flicked on. It was Mrs. Roopy, standing in the doorway looking at us.

"What's the meaning of this?" she asked.

She had her hands on her hips, so we knew she was mad. For some reason, grown-ups always put their hands on their hips when they are mad.

"I had nothing to do with it!" Andrea said. "It was all A.J.'s idea!"

Everybody was looking at me. I had to think fast. I didn't want to spend the rest of my life in jail.

I grabbed George Washington's uniform out of the closet.

"What's the meaning of . . . *this*?" I said, holding up the costume. "You told us you were home sick in bed and George Washington was here instead of you. How do you explain the fact that George

Washington's uniform is in your closet? Huh?"

We all turned to look at Mrs. Roopy.

She just stood there for a moment and then . . . she broke down crying. She was sobbing and big tears were running down her face. It was so sad that we all gathered around her and gave her a hug. Emily was crying too.

"This is horrible!" Mrs. Roopy said, wiping her eyes with a tissue.

"You'll be okay, Mrs. Roopy," Andrea said. "We'll get you some help."

"No, it's horrible!" Mrs. Roopy cried. "George Washington must have left his uniform in my closet when he was here.

Do you know what this means?"

"What?"

"It means George Washington is running around somewhere with no clothes on!"

Just Admit It!

It was no use. Even after we proved to Mrs. Roopy that she was dressing up as all these characters, she still wouldn't admit it.

"Mrs. Roopy is in denial," Andrea said when we got back to the classroom. "I'll bet you don't know what that means, A.J."

"Sure I know what 'denial' means," I said. "It's that river in Africa."

"Not the Nile, dumbhead! Denial! It means she can't admit to herself that she has a problem."

"So what are we supposed to do now?" Michael asked.

"There's only one thing we can do," Andrea said. "We've got to tell Mr. Klutz."

Mr. Klutz is the principal, which means he is like the king of the school. One time I got into trouble and was sent to Mr. Klutz's office. When I got there, he didn't punish me. He gave me a candy bar. Mr. Klutz is nuts!

We told Miss Daisy that we had to speak with Mr. Klutz and that it was a matter of life and death. She called the office and in a few minutes Mr. Klutz arrived.

Mr. Klutz has no hair at all. We told him all about the crazy things Mrs. Roopy had been doing and how Andrea's mother is a psychologist and she thinks Mrs. Roopy might have a big problem.

"We're really worried about her," Emily said.

"Hmmm, this sounds pretty serious," Mr. Klutz said. "Maybe we'd better go have a little chat with Mrs. Roopy."

Mr. Klutz led us down the hall to the library. When

we got there, Mrs. Roopy was lying on the floor under the tree house. She was holding her head like it had been hit. Not only that, but Mrs. Roopy was really fat. It looked like she had gained about a million hundred pounds!

"What happened, Mrs. Roopy?" Michael asked. "Are you okay?"

"Mrs. Roopy? Who's that?" Mrs. Roopy said. "My name is Humpty Dumpty. I was sitting on that wall up there, and I had a great fall."

"Don't tell me," Andrea said. "All the king's horses and all the king's men couldn't put you back together again. Right?"

"How did you know?" Mrs. Roopy asked.

"You're not Humpty Dumpty!" Andrea said. "You're Mrs. Roopy, our librarian! Just admit it!"

"It doesn't matter who it is," Mr. Klutz said. "There has been an injury. I need to write a report and give it to the Board of Education."

"You can give it to me," I told Mr. Klutz.

"I'm bored of education."

Everybody laughed even though I didn't say anything funny. Mr. Klutz said he had to go call a doctor for Humpty Dumpty. Mrs. Roopy got up off the floor and dusted herself off.

"Wait a minute," I said. "I have a question."

"Yes, A.J.?" asked Mrs. Roopy.

"Your name is Humpty Dumpty, right?"

"Right."

"What I want to know is, why did your parents name you Humpty? I mean, if their last name was already Dumpty, they could have named you John or Jim or Joe or something normal. But they had to go and name you Humpty?"

"Well, actually, Humpty is just my nick-name," Mrs. Roopy said. "My real name is Lumpy."

"Lumpy Dumpty?" I said.

"Yes," said Mrs. Roopy. "So you can see why I'd rather be called Humpty."

Andrea was getting all angry now. Mrs. Roopy was simply not going to admit she wasn't Humpty Dumpty.

"Nursery Rhyme Week is over, Mrs. Roopy!" Andrea said. "You can be your-self. You can stop pretending to be other people."

"Don't you like nursery rhymes?" asked Mrs. Roopy.

"Sure I do," Andrea said. "But enough is enough!"

"I hate nursery rhymes!" I said. "Nursery rhymes are dumb. I'm sick of nursery rhymes. Nursery rhymes are boring."

Humpty, I mean, Mrs. Roopy, looked hurt.

"Everything is boring to you, A.J.," she said sadly. "I've tried so hard not to bore you. Please. Tell me. What is not boring to you?"

I put on my thinking cap (well, not really) and tried real hard to think of something that wasn't boring.

"Trick bikes," I said. "Trick bikes aren't boring."

The Proof

It was the middle of our afternoon snack time. I traded my pretzel sticks with Ryan for his cup of chocolate pudding. Suddenly I heard somebody yelling down the hallway.

"Watch out! Coming through! Out of the way!"

"I wonder what that could be," said Miss Daisy.

The yelling got louder. Everybody in the class turned around just in time to see somebody ride into our classroom on a trick bike.

It was Mrs. Roopy! She was wearing sunglasses, knee pads, elbow pads, and a floppy black T-shirt that said "Bikers 4 Books." She had combed her hair to make it stick up all spiky.

"Hey, dudes!" she said as she skidded to a stop right in front of my desk. "I just landed an awesomely tweaked tailwhip with a Superman seat grab to a toothpick grind. You should have seen it! It was really sick!"

Everybody put down their snacks and gathered around my desk to look at Mrs. Roopy's cool bike.

"I didn't know you knew so much about trick biking, Mrs. Roopy," I said.

"I'm not Mrs. Roopy," Mrs. Roopy said.

"I'm a professional trick biker!"

"You are not!" we all hollered. "You're Mrs. Roopy, the librarian!"

"Am not!"

"Are too!"

"It certainly looks like a trick biker to me," said Miss Daisy.

That's when I came up with the most genius idea in the history of the world. Mrs. Roopy's tattoo! I remembered that she had a picture of a heart on her belly button!

"You're Mrs. Roopy," I said, grabbing the bottom of her T-shirt, "and I can prove it!"

"Oh, stop that!" Mrs. Roopy giggled. "I'm ticklish!"

When I yanked at her shirt, three books fell out. One of them hit my snack on my desk. The cup of chocolate pudding went flying. It splashed all over Mrs. Roopy's tummy. It almost covered up the tattoo of a heart, but we could still see it.

"It's Mrs. Roopy!" Michael shouted. "The proof is in the pudding!"

"Hey!" Ryan shouted. "Check out these books!" Ryan picked up the books that had dropped on the floor. They were books about trick biking! One of the books showed how to do tricks, and the other two were about famous trick bikers. Cool!

"I didn't know they made books about trick biking," Ryan said.

"So that's how you know so much about trick biking, Mrs. Roopy!" I said.

"I don't know what you're talking about," Mrs. Roopy said. "I'm a professional trick biker."

"Can I check these books out of the

library?" asked Michael.

"No, I get them first," Ryan said.

"Hey, I was the one who found them," I said.

Miss Daisy grabbed all the books.

"Gee, I don't know, A.J.," she said. "You said that reading was boring, so you probably wouldn't want to read these books."

"Yes I would!" I shouted. "Pleeeeease?"

"Well, okay," Miss Daisy said as she handed each of us one of the trick bike books. "But if you don't bring these back on time, Mrs. Roopy is going to lock you in the dungeon on the third floor."

We all looked at Mrs. Roopy.

"Later, dudes!" she said. And with that,

Mrs. Roopy went pedaling out into the hallway.

I feel sorry for Mrs. Roopy. She is the loopiest librarian I've ever met. I think she's got a big problem. We're going to do all we can to help her. But it won't be easy.

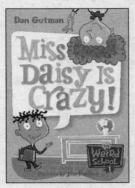

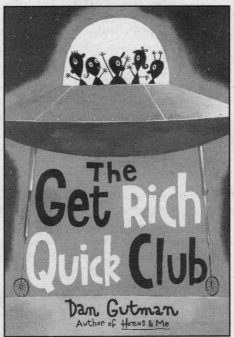